This book belongs to

_____

Diversity

Bear In Mind Series

For permissions contact:
info@littlehippobooks.com

ISBN: 978-1-956818-19-2

Illustrations by Marc Mones
Written by Karen Nespoli

First printing edition 2022.

Little Hippo Books
www.littlehippobooks.com

BEAR iN MiND
DIVERSITY

Illustrated by
Marc Mones

Written by
Karen Nespoli

Tips for reading with children:

Follow these tips to help keep your child engaged during story time.

- Have fun while you read! Use different voices for the different characters.

- Ask questions about the pages you just read.

- Point out fun objects in the art.

- Have a routine. Try to read with children at the same time each day.

"Let's have a race from here to that tree," challenged Diversity Bear.

"You know I can run faster than you," replied Inclusion Bear.

"Ready, Set, Go," shouted Diversity Bear.

Inclusion Bear started racing toward the tree and was
out in front in no time. Suddenly, both bears stopped when
they saw their friend sitting on a bench looking sad.

"No one wants to play with me because
I am different," sighed Creative Bear.

"Those bears told me that I look funny because my fur is not the same color and that I cannot play with them. They hurt my feelings."

"They don't want us to play with them either,"
added two other bears.
"Only bears with fur like theirs could play with them."

"I am sorry that the other bears did not include you in their bear games. They need to learn that being different is a paws-itive thing," explained Diversity Bear. "Being different makes us special and unique."

"Inclusion Bear and I are best friends.
Our fur is very different and we **accept** that we are different.
Some bears want everyone to be the same."

"What a boring world this would be if we were all exactly the same," shared Inclusion Bear.

"We both love pizza and reading books,
but we also like different things.
I like baseball and Inclusion Bear likes basketball.

Inclusion Bear likes to draw and I like to play the drums.
Our differences make us special," Diversity Bear pointed out.

Diversity means differences.
We are different in many ways.

We may look different.
We may talk or communicate in
different ways.

We may like different things
or eat different foods,
but we are all **bears.**

"The color of our fur should not
be a reason to treat us differently.

When other bears do not **accept** our different colored fur it is not right. Someone should not be treated unfairly because of how they look."

"When I see someone who is alone, it makes me sad,"
said Inclusion Bear. "It is important to me
that everyone feels **accepted** and no one is left out.

First, I try to think about how the other bear feels and try to make them feel more accepted. Then, I start by being friendly and saying nice things to the bear. I try to show all bears **compassion** by trying to help them."

"I get it now," shared Creative Bear.
"If we practice acceptance and compassion,
no bears will have hurt feelings or feel left out."

"That's right," agreed Diversity Bear. "Acceptance and compassion are very important in this very **diverse** world."

"I have an idea," blurted Creative Bear.
"We can start a Beary Special Club where all bears are welcome and we will never leave anyone behind.

In this club we can celebrate our differences
and share how our differences make us special and unique.
Who wants to join our Club?"

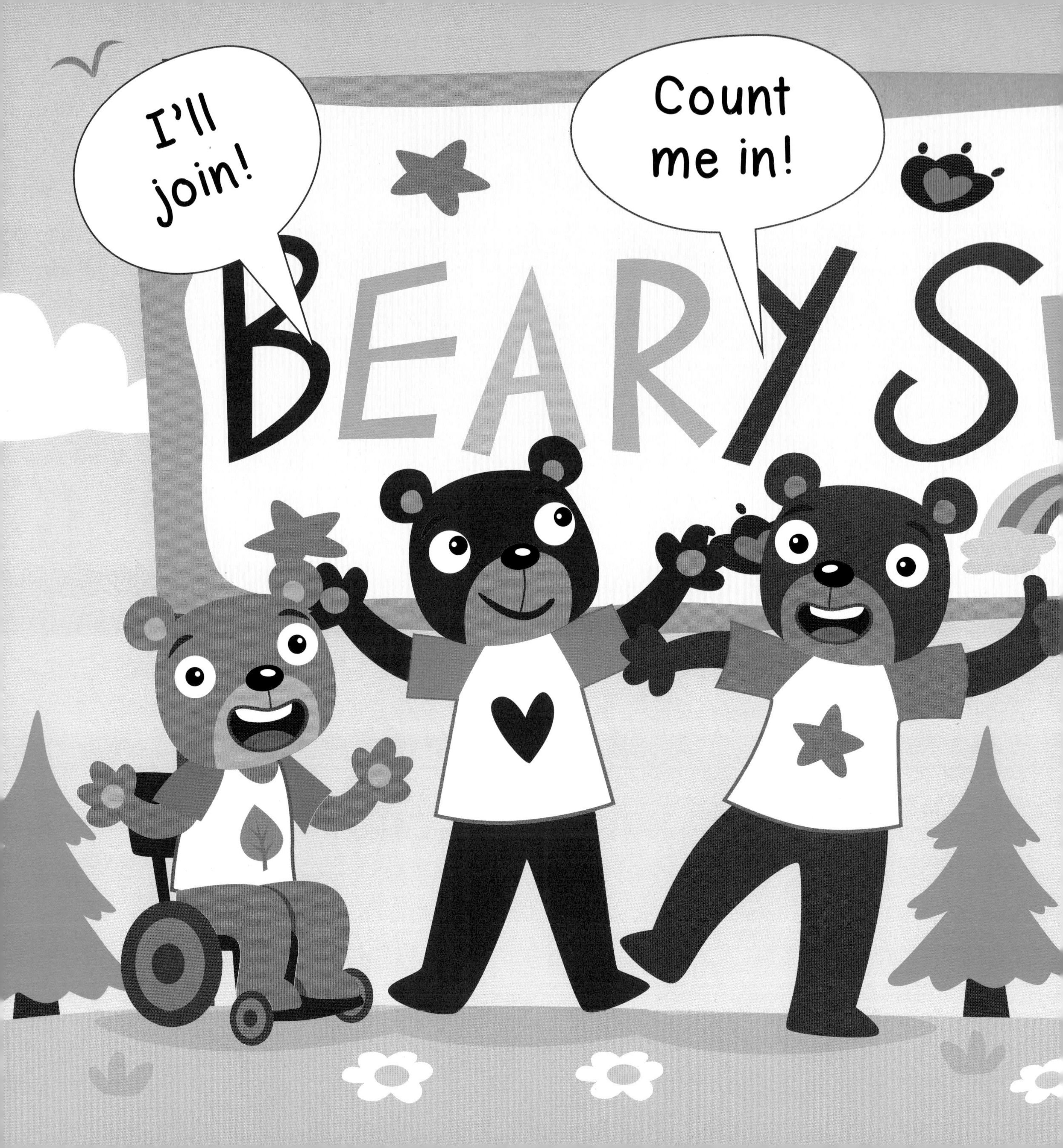
I'll join!
Count me in!
BEARY S

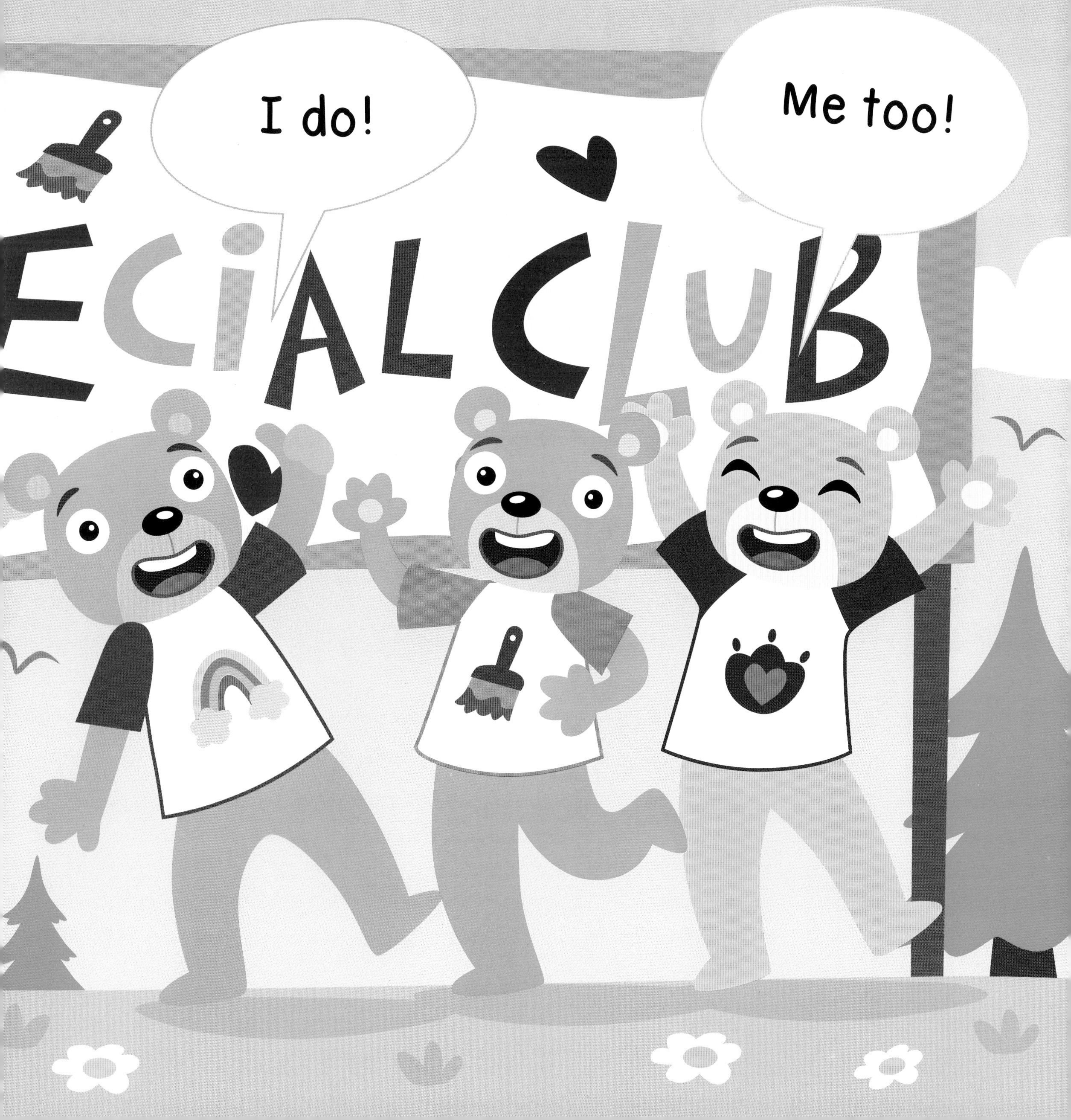
I do!
Me too!
ECIAL CLUB

"Would you like to join our Beary Special Club?
We can start by getting to know what makes YOU special."

"All you need is a little paws-itive thinking and the activity on the next page to get started," shared Diversity Bear.

What Makes Me Special
Diversity Bear

Eye Color: Black

Hair Color: Green

Skin Color: Green

Favorite Food: Pizza

Favorite Hobby: Playing Drums

Favorite Book: Bear In Mind

Favorite Game: Baseball

Favorite Family Tradition: Spaghetti Night

What Makes Me Special Activity

Materials:

Construction Paper

Markers or Crayons

Directions:

For this activity you will create a

What Makes 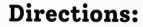 **Special Chart.**

(Put your name in the blank spot.)

Next, write the answers to the following:

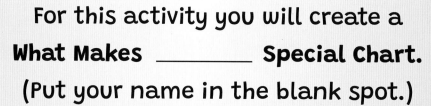

Eye Color	Favorite Hobby
Hair Color	Favorite Book
Skin Color	Favorite Game
Favorite Food	Favorite Family Tradition

What Makes Me Special

Diversity Bear

Eye Color: Black

Hair Color: Green

Skin Color: Green

Favorite Food: Pizza

Favorite Hobby: Playing Drums

Favorite Book: Bear In Mind

Favorite Game: Baseball

Favorite Family Tradition: Spaghetti Night

You can keep this chart in your room and
always remember how special you are.
Then ask a friend or family member to answer
the questions and compare your lists.
You will learn some things about your friends
and family that make them special.
This will help you practice acceptance.
This is also a great activity for the Beary Special Club to try.

A Guide For
Parents and Teachers

We all know it is sometimes difficult
to discuss topics such as Diversity and Inclusion
with young children. Here are some ideas to help:

What Makes Me Special
Diversity Bear
Eye Color: Black
Hair Color: Green
Skin Color: Green
Favorite Food: Pizza
Favorite Hobby: Playing Drums
Favorite Book: Bear In Mind
Favorite Game: Baseball
Favorite Family Tradition: Spaghetti Night

Discuss what things make your
child special and unique. Create the
What Makes Me Special chart with your
child and share the things you see that
make your child special.

Teach children that asking questions is an important part of understanding differences. If a child is using a wheel chair, help them to understand how that wheel chair makes them special.

Introduce your child to different cultures. Sharing books, music, art, dance and exposing your child to different languages will help them be more accepting.

Discussion Questions About Diversity for Children

Encourage children to think about the diversity in their lives. Through these questions you can validate to your child that, yes, everyone is different and that is ok.

What makes YOU different?

1. Do YOU sometimes feel different? Maybe from your friends? Maybe from your siblings or relatives?

2. Do you think anyone else you know feels different too? Maybe a friend? Or someone you don't talk to in school?

3. How would it feel to live in a world where everything is the same?

4. What makes you feel different from those around you?

5. How does it feel knowing that you are different?

6. Can feeling different ever be a good thing? How so?

About The Author

Karen Nespoli completed her Ed.D. in Curriculum and Instruction with an emphasis on Literacy and the Education of the Gifted at Teachers College, Columbia University. She received her B.A. from Queens College (CUNY) in elementary education, and her M.S. degree from Queens College (CUNY) in Special Education. She also holds two Professional Diplomas from St. John's University in Administration and Supervision and Educational Leadership.

Karen Patricia Nespoli, Ed.D.

Karen Nespoli's background includes working as an elementary school teacher in the New York Public Schools, and as a Gifted Education Consultant on Long Island. She is the former Literacy Professor and Director of the Literacy and Cognition Program at St. Joseph's College.

Karen Nespoli is the author of two online professional development programs with Scenario Learning, namely, Early Childhood: Language Development and Literacy and Gifted Learners and Differentiated Instruction.

Karen Nespoli was born and raised in Queens, New York. She now makes her home with her husband on Long Island. She has two married daughters. When Karen is not writing children's stories she can be found walking along the beach collecting small shells and other treasures. Karen loves to bake and her favorite is chocolate chip cookies. She enjoys a nice hot cup of tea and a good mystery book.

As a former elementary school teacher and literacy educator, Karen has guided children to write and illustrate stories. Now, through her books and website, she hopes to inspire, challenge and encourage children to grow as writers.

Check out her website at Karennespoli.com
You can also find Karen on Twitter and Instagram @drkarenn

DIVERSITY DIPLOMA

This certificate is presented to

_____

Name

For completion of diversity and inclusion
educational activities.

_____

Date

_____

Signature

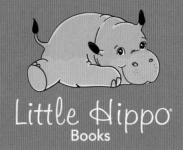

Little Hippo
Books

Sign up to see what's new at
littlehippobooks.com.

Follow us on social media to stay up to date
on the latest from Little Hippo Books.

 @LittleHippoBooks

 @LittleHippoBooks

 Little Hippo Books